I0700399

Undead

unDEAD

Mae MacCallum

Undead by Mae MacCallum
Copyright © 2023 by Mae MacCallum
All rights reserved.

ISBN: 979-8-218-07893-5

Published by Rotten Pumpkin Press
https://rottenpumpkinpress.com

Cover Design by Innsanctum Designs

Edited by Nia Quinn at https://editor.niaquinn.com/

No part of this publication may be reproduced, stored in a retrieval system, or transmitted in any form or by any means, without the prior written permission of the publisher, nor be otherwise circulated in any form of binding or cover than that in which it is published and without a similar condition including this condition being imposed on the subsequent purchaser.

This is a work of fiction and any names, characters, businesses, places, events, and incidents are either fictional or used in a fictitious manner. Any resemblance to actual persons, living or dead, or actual events is purely coincidental.

This story contains:

Gun Violence, Mass Shootings, Kidnapping, Death, Murder, Decapitation, Mutilation of Corpses, and Cutting of Limbs.

Reader discretion is advised.

Hey! rub-a-dub, ho! rub-a-dub, three maids in a tub,
And who do you think were there?
The butcher, the baker, the candlestick-maker,
And all of them gone to the fair.

MONDAY

Claudia was dead. She could see her body on the ground over there. A puddle of blood spread over the beige carpet. She'd been shot in the back. She hadn't realized until she had gotten home and started to bleed all over the floor.

The day Claudia died seemed like it would be a normal day, until Claudia went to the grocery store after work. Before walking down the frozen foods aisle where her life would change completely, her day at the office had been as mundanely miserable as every other day.

Claudia worked as a legal assistant at a law firm that handled estate law. The office took up the entire twenty-seventh floor in a nice, corporate-looking building. Law firms, psychiatrists' offices, and a matchmaking service occupied the rest of the building. It had a cavernous white lobby with a few green potted plants here and there. Everyone's footsteps echoed when they walked through. The law office where Claudia worked shared the style of the rest of the building, with white walls, oak desks, new computers, and gray carpet. The partners expected everyone to match the scenery to keep the wealthy clients at ease.

Claudia's boss, Moira, owned the business. Moira was a stern and intimidating middle-aged woman with a tall build, dark hair, pale skin, and a humorless expression. She refused to treat her frown lines with Botox, not concerned that she looked permanently displeased. Moira enjoyed intimidating her employees and clients when she entered a room and wore tailored black suit dresses and kept her hair tied up tight. Moira talked to most people slowly and carefully like they were children she was deeply frustrated with. People around the office treated her with quiet respect and gave her a wide berth. Claudia had a knack for angering Moira.

Claudia had been hired as a legal assistant, but she had become more like the office's go-to person, *almost like an office manager*, Claudia told herself. Claudia was Moira's person to ask for coffee, get lunch for everyone, clean the conference room, and do trivial office tasks the rest of the employees were too busy to do. Other legal assistants, like Chrissy, did more of the actual legal work: proofreading, finding contract errors, and filing documents. Still, Claudia figured everyone had a role that suited them. And Claudia's role had been to make sure the office ran smoothly so the job could get done. Claudia often received Moira's slowest and lowest voice even though she never let the coffee station run out of filters and she always kept the supply closet stocked with the pens the office preferred.

Only a few men worked there, including Elliot, Moira's second-in-command. A wealthy, good-looking man in his midthirties, he seemed happy and almost carefree, like he had never endured any real hardship. Elliot's warmth and charm stood out beside cold, clinical Moira. With blond hair and blue eyes, he kept himself impeccably dressed, and had the air of availability. The women in the office fawned over him. The older clients did as well.

The morning of the day Claudia died, she had somehow managed to forget it was Chrissy's birthday. Moira was already in the room when Claudia got to her desk. Moira glanced from Claudia's empty hands to her purse with only her lunch inside.

"Do you think you'll have time to go to the store before the meeting?"

"What?"

Moira sighed.

"It is Chrissy's birthday. Did you forget? We need to have a celebration today that makes her feel appreciated and raises morale, and it must be cleaned up before Mr. Abberline arrives at one o'clock."

"Oh crap. I must have forgotten."

"Go. Now," Moira said, stomping back to her office.

Claudia picked up her bag and went to the grocery store. She needed to get drinks, some light snacks, a cake for Chrissy, and a smaller nut-free dessert Bailey could eat. On the way she would have to call and order lunch for the office. She rushed through the store to get everything and was halfway back to the office when she remembered they were out of paper plates.

Claudia was upset she had forgotten it was Chrissy's birthday. Usually, she was on top of details like this. Claudia managed the office well without anyone having to remind her of anything. She didn't want to give Moira any more reason to dislike her. Everyone liked Chrissy, especially Moira. Claudia personally thought Chrissy was rude and pushy, and that she had no right to be that way, being the youngest person in the office. But Chrissy had been rewarded for her bad behavior by being given the largest workload, with Moira often telling her she was the "only person I can trust not to mess this up."

Claudia had forgotten Chrissy's birthday because she had a lot on her mind. Claudia had been having anxiety dreams about bills she couldn't pay, about showing up to work with holes in her clothes and everyone laughing at her. She had intended to ask Moira for a raise today, but she probably shouldn't ask now, after forgetting. Maybe if she could pull the party off, it would be okay.

Claudia hurried back to the office and set up for the party in record time. She even wrote Chrissy's name on the cake in pink frosting herself. It all looked nice. As soon as lunch was delivered, she gathered everyone in the conference room for cake and coffee, snacks, seltzers, and mocktails. It seemed like Chrissy was pleased. Then Claudia cleaned up and returned the conference room to its pristine state. She had twenty minutes to spare before Mr. Abberline arrived.

The conference room tidy, Claudia nodded to herself. She would ask Moira for the raise, now. She had come through on the party, and Moira would be in too bad of a mood after Mr. Abberline left to talk about it then. It was now or never. And Claudia needed a raise immediately.

Claudia entered Moira's office quietly.

"Is the conference room ready?" Moira asked, not glancing up from the papers on her desk.

"Yes, all cleaned up, and I have coffee brewing and refreshments laid out for Mr. Abberline's arrival. But I wondered if I could ask you something?"

Moira gazed unflinchingly into Claudia's eyes. Claudia stared down at the floor in front of Moira's desk.

"I wanted to ask if I could have a raise?"

"Do you think you deserve a raise?" Moira asked, her expression unchanged.

"Yes?"

"List instances in which your performance or your workload exceeded what I have come to expect from you," Moira said.

"Well, today I was able to—"

"Don't say it's because you set up a birthday party. A clown can do that," Moira interrupted her. "Give me a real reason."

"Um, well, I—"

"Try harder, and maybe I'll consider it."

"I really need more money now," Claudia mumbled. Moira laughed. Claudia couldn't remember if she had ever heard her laugh before.

"That's not my problem."

Claudia left Moira's office with her face red. She went to double-check the conference room was ready for the meeting.

Mr. Abberline arrived at precisely one o'clock for his estate-planning meeting with Moira and Elliot to work through his large complicated will. A tad eccentric, he only wore bright-colored suits, each perfectly tailored to his short, round body. The day Claudia died, he sported a bright green suit. Claudia smirked—he looked a little bit like a leprechaun. Mr. Abberline's visits were always chaotic and disorganized. His personality didn't reflect how cheerfully he dressed, and he tended to be gruff with most people. His dislike for Elliot was evident, but nothing compared to his loathing for Moira. Out of everyone, he only treated Claudia with kindness.

Claudia showed Mr. Abberline into the conference room and brought him a cup of decaf coffee with cream and no sugar. She helped him arrange his papers and took a seat next to him at the conference table while Moira and Elliot joined them on the other side. Chrissy perched in a chair in the corner, ready to type notes on her laptop.

Mr. Abberline's daughter had passed away in a car accident in her twenties. When he first met Claudia, he told her she reminded him of his daughter. He wanted only Claudia to sit next to him during the meetings, to help him organize his papers and take notes for him. Sometimes he would get so frustrated with Moira, he would pass notes to Claudia and have her answer on his behalf.

Normally, Moira would seethe and smile and allow this behavior to continue for as long as the client wanted (he was paying for the time, after all), but it had become clear they were running out of time. Each time Mr. Abberline came to the office, his hands trembled more, his skin was paler, and his breaths were louder. They needed to get his estate settled before he passed. Something they couldn't seem to agree on, however, was the treasure hunt.

"I want this portion of my estate to go to the winner of the treasure hunt! I don't know what's difficult for you to understand about that!" Mr. Abberline huffed at Moira for the sixth time.

"It's not how estates are handled, Mr. Abberline," Moira said. "It's not professional. And with that amount of money, it is inappropriate."

"Could we limit the amount for the winner of the hunt?" Elliot asked.

"Absolutely not," Mr. Abberline said. "The treasure has already been hidden."

Moira clenched her jaw, and Elliot looked at her, the smile momentarily gone from his face.

"The full five million?"

"And I'll give you the clues everyone else is going to get, but not the answers."

"And why not?"

"I don't want you getting there before anyone else. You're a smart lady, though—I bet you could figure it out if you tried."

"I need to know where you've hidden the assets, Mr. Abberline."

After two weeks of this same conversation, they were at a standstill.

Today—the day Claudia died—things got especially heated in the meeting with Mr. Abberline and Moira. Claudia thought Moira was pushing him because he looked so unwell. He kept patting his clammy forehead with a kerchief, and he wheezed more than usual. Moira and Elliot departed the conference room to take a break, with Chrissy announcing she was going to get more coffee, leaving Mr. Abberline and Claudia alone.

"She doesn't understand," he said.

"Why a treasure hunt?" Claudia asked.

"I once read about someone hiding a treasure and giving the public clues to find it. I liked the idea."

"I remember something like that. Didn't it take people years to find it?"

"Oh yes, and people died looking for it."

"And that's what you want?"

He smiled. "For five million, some people can die. It's part of the intrigue! It has to be a little dangerous." He began to cough, covering his mouth with his kerchief, sweat glistening between the folds of skin on his forehead. "I don't have much time left," he said slowly and softly. "I have no children now, no wife. All I have is a few distant relatives and all this money. I have no legacy."

"The game would give you a legacy?"

"People would talk about it for years!" He laughed. "It would be something to remember me by."

"Why can't Moira have the answers? Even just by putting the information into an envelope and sealing it in front of witnesses so she can't see the answer. No one would have to know."

"If the answer is out there, and anyone finds out, they'll go after that instead of playing the game. Especially my distant relatives. It ruins all the fun."

"What if you just told it to someone?"

"I don't know if I can trust anyone that way."

"But what happens if . . ."

"If I die suddenly?" He sighed. "I've been trying not to think about it."

"Are you afraid?"

"I'll be alone when it happens. I worry I'll be alone after it's over as well. I'm not sure what is going to happen, but if I thought I was going to be reunited with loved ones, if I knew it in my gut, then I wouldn't be afraid. But I am. I'm terrified to die."

"I would be afraid too," Claudia said. "If I died tomorrow, I would leave behind such a big mess for my mother."

"What kind of a mess?" he asked.

"Financial," Claudia said.

Mr. Abberline studied Claudia closely. His sweaty brow furrowed, and his eyes looked far away, like he was remembering something from long ago.

"You look so much like my Jubilee," he said. "And you've been so kind to me even though I'm being difficult."

"My father left when I was little. I don't remember him very well. But I bet you were a wonderful father to her, while she was here."

"I tried," he sighed. "I just don't want it to all be for nothing."

"Even if you don't get your treasure hunt, I'll never forget you." Claudia smiled at him.

His eyes started to glisten, and his lips trembled for a moment. He took a deep, shaky breath.

"Will you lean closer so I can tell you something?"

Claudia leaned over to the old man, and he whispered in her ear. As he was whispering, Moira and Elliot returned to the conference room. Mr. Abberline looked flustered and pointed at Moira, shouting, "I won't give away the hiding spot!"

He deflated, skin wan, and turned to Claudia. "Would you please wheel me to the elevator so I can leave?"

Moira smirked as they left.

After Mr. Abberline was gone, Moira cornered Claudia cleaning up coffee cups in the conference room.

"What did the old man say to you?" she asked, getting closer to Claudia than she liked.

"Nothing, just some dirty stuff," Claudia said. Moira studied her, as though trying to deduce if she was lying or not, watching Claudia until she left the room.

After work, Claudia went to the grocery store to buy dinner—her third trip today. She shook her head in annoyance. In the frozen foods section, she looked over individual meals, trying to decide what she should get. How long after Mr. Abberline died should she wait to find his treasure and fix her life?

Gunshots erupted through the store.

*

When Claudia was eight, she saw a boy kidnapped in front of her. She had just gotten off the school bus with Benjamin Howard. Everyone called him Benny. They were in the same class and lived a few houses away from each other.

After the bus pulled away, a white car drove up to them. The car rattled loudly, the music from the radio turned up. A man from the car came up behind Benny. He put his hand over Benny's mouth and dragged him into the backseat of the car. A woman smirked in the driver's seat, and once the man and Benny were in the back, the car sped off.

Claudia had just stood there and watched it happen. She hadn't known what to do.

*

After the gunshots and the screaming, police officers ushered Claudia out of the store, where paramedics were standing by, shouting to the injured to come to them. Claudia wandered to their voices.

A young man asked her if she was injured, and she just stared at him blankly. He informed her he was going to touch her body, gently lifted her arms, and looked at her, checking for wounds or injuries. He confirmed she was okay and asked her to sit on the curb over there until she started to feel better. Claudia sat and obeyed. Eventually, the numbness that had overtaken her mind faded, so she dropped the blanket to the ground and rushed to her car.

Once home, Claudia locked her apartment door. Something was wrong. She fell to her knees, unable to breathe. Her head was spinning, and nothing in the room would come into focus. She touched her chest, her fingers coming away damp. She raised her hand, her skin stained red with blood. Struggling to breathe, she fell to the ground, chills overtaking her as her blood poured out. Barely able to move, she tried to reach her phone but couldn't. Her mouth sputtered and gasped. Eventually, everything went black, only her gasps and strange chokes disrupting the nothingness. Then it was like she fell asleep.

*

Claudia woke up standing above her dead body. She tried to think how this could have happened. The paramedic had checked her. But he'd checked her quickly, and she had been wearing black. But why hadn't she started bleeding until she got inside? Why not during the car ride home? Maybe adrenaline or shock could explain that somehow.

She looked at her body. A huge pool of blood all around her had soaked into the beige carpet. She still had her car keys clutched in her white hand. How this had happened didn't matter, because it was all over. She was dead.

Claudia turned away from her body. A door that hadn't been there before stood in her living room—a heavy silver door with a latch, like the door to an industrial freezer. It was just there, as though it had always been there. Claudia swayed forward. This must be where you went after you died. The door must lead to the afterlife or heaven or whatever there was. Without thinking about it, Claudia tiptoed to the door and opened it.

She found herself in a large bone-chilling refrigerator. A cloud of cold air spilled out from a metal grate in the ceiling. The walls and floor—everything—was white except the skinned carcasses hanging from hooks. Blood spills and splatters stained the otherwise shiny floor. Claudia stared at the hanging bodies for a moment before stumbling back in horror. They were human.

Chop.

Chop.

Chop.

She peered around the corner through the frigid blowing mist. A huge man worked at a steel table, wider than any man should be. He wore only a white apron tied around his neck and back, otherwise nude. Deep scars marked his blue-tinged skin from head to toe, as though he had been slashed and cut many times over. His large cleaver rose and fell, chopping something meaty. Claudia stared for a moment. His cleaver split something in two.

Chop.

Chop.

Chop.

He was cutting up a *leg*. Splatters of blood fluttered through the air as he chopped the leg into slices, skin still intact. There was no pooling of red fluids or steam rising from the appendage as it was diced up, it was so cold in the freezer. He stopped his work and set the cleaver down. Terror shot through Claudia that he would turn around, that at any moment he would see her, and she would have to look at what had to be an ugly and horrible face.

Claudia whirled and exited the fridge through the door she'd come in. She found herself back in her living room. Her dead body still lay on the floor, the blood still pooling. It was still night outside. When she looked behind her, the refrigerator door had disappeared.

She shuddered. Had she rejected the afterlife? She had read once that ghosts were spirits who refused to cross over after they died. Perhaps that was what she had just done. She must be a ghost now.

Claudia didn't know how long she would be dead. Or rather, how long she would be able to stay in the apartment with her body. She didn't know what she was now. Grief engulfed her, like she was chok-ing on her blood all over again. She thought of the life she wouldn't get to lead: a husband, children, her poor mother, reconciliation with her father, birth-days, weddings, graduations, and baptisms. She couldn't cry, so she moaned. She moaned into the night.

TUESDAY

Claudia watched the sunrise from her apartment window. She only had one window in the living room where she could see the sunrise in all its glory. At the rest of the windows, tall buildings blocked the view. Her apartment was nice enough, but she wished she had been able to afford a better view. She had already paid dearly for this one.

As the sun appeared, Claudia stopped moaning. The waves of grief receded long enough that she could think. The light of the sun touched her body on the floor and gave her skin an almost peachy glow. She was still dead. She wasn't sure what to do now. Being dead felt like being in a dream, or sleepwalking: real and not real at the same time. Claudia still felt like herself, but now very much apart from the rest of the world. Where were the other dead people?

Claudia had considered if her father was dead. If he was dead, he might be here to greet her and guide her into the afterlife. But he had left her and her mother when she was a child, so maybe he had chosen to be absent in her afterlife as well. There was no way to know for sure. Would she be there for her mother when she passed?

She glided to her bedroom, feeling light, almost airy. Piles of clothes with the tags still on cluttered the floor. Folded and crumpled shopping bags littered the corners. She looked in the mirror. She could see herself. She didn't look translucent, as she imagined a ghost would, but almost like she was glowing. Like she was composed of more energy than she normally was. And to her surprise, she was naked. She didn't feel the cold or the discomfort of being naked.

Opening her closet, which was bursting full of clothing, purses, and shoes, she was surprised again that she could open the door at all. She would have thought a ghost would pass through doors. Claudia changed into her favorite outfit: a cream dress, and a pink blazer. She donned her pearl necklace and gold earrings with ease. Her ghost feet slipped into nude flats.

Her rent was due today, she remembered suddenly. She looked at the stack of credit card bills and the overdrawn bank statements on her vanity. It didn't matter anymore. It was all meaningless.

Claudia toyed with the gold button on her blazer. Was death like being reborn? Was she new in the world again? Like a fresh start. She looked at herself in the mirror, dressed nicely and slightly glowing.

She felt better. Life had taken its toll on her. She hadn't realized how heavy a burden it had all been until it was gone and she was free of it.

What did she want to do now? She nodded to herself. She'd go to work, maybe for the last time. She would walk among her former coworkers and say goodbye to her life. Maybe she would whisper to Mr. Abberline that death wasn't so bad and hope he could hear her. Maybe she would try to play a ghost trick on Moira—not too serious, of course. Maybe she would kiss Elliot. Maybe she would follow him home and see what his apartment looked like.

Visiting her mother would be too sad and painful. Just thinking about it made her want to wail. She didn't want to scare her mother. The last time she had seen her mother was at brunch last Sunday. It had been so nice. They had talked about nothing significant, maybe a show they were both watching, and had eggs and a few mimosas. Claudia had made a big show of paying for the outing with a credit card. She loved being able to take care of her mother. And that was a good last memory to have with her. She didn't want a different one where her mother was afraid or sad or depressed. She wanted to remember her at brunch that last time.

And maybe that final act of saying goodbye to her daily routine at work would be enough. Maybe that would allow her to pass into the afterlife, or whatever was meant to happen after this. There had to be somewhere else she could go besides that cold refrigerator with that man and his cleaver. Claudia couldn't imagine this, or even that, was all there was of death.

Claudia had to pry her car keys out of her cold, dead fingers. It was harder than she'd thought it would be. Would she even be able to drive the car? She pressed the button to unlock the doors. She started the car. Would her ability to manipulate physical things in the world fade the longer she was dead?

She drove slowly and carefully. She didn't want to get pulled over or get into an accident as a ghost. Not like she could die again, though. She thought about maybe doing something crazy on purpose—jumping in front of a train, or off the top of a building. But that would be too scary, even as a ghost.

When Claudia got to her office, it was like any other Tuesday morning. The security guard didn't look up as she passed through the lobby. No one seemed to notice her or step aside to make room for her when she got on the elevator. Claudia took this as confirmation no one could see her.

She entered the law firm and walked around the office. No one looked at her or said good morning. Everyone stood around Chrissy's desk, talking about the shooting at the grocery store last night.

Claudia's mind dredged up the horror of last night: blood on a white linoleum floor, screaming and loud pops. She winced and then shuddered. She didn't want those memories. She pushed them away.

Her coworkers talked about the shooter being taken into custody and the people already listed as victims. Should she try to whisper to one of them that she was a victim too? They wouldn't know what had happened to her for a while. Not until someone realized she was missing and checked her apartment. How long might that take? And even then, they might think it was a home invasion or something. They wouldn't know who had shot her. Something about that felt unfair.

Moira walked by with her face in a file. She glanced up at the group. She returned her attention to the file and said, "Claudia, can you bring a cup of coffee to my desk? We have a conference call with the Abberline estate in fifteen minutes."

Claudia didn't move.

"Claudia, now," Moira said, walking away.

The others stopped talking and stared at Claudia like they were waiting for her. They could all see her. She hadn't been invisible at all. Her hopes of haunting them dashed, how could she still take advantage of being dead while at the office? She deserved to have a little fun before she left forever.

Claudia poured Moira's coffee. Why could people

see her? Maybe it was because she hadn't been dead for very long? Maybe it was like those stories where someone had a conversation with a ghost and didn't realize until later. They just didn't know she was dead. Claudia didn't want to tell them. Not yet.

They all waited in the conference room for the meeting to start. Two distant cousins of Mr. Abberline appeared on a screen at the head of the table.

"Mr. Abberline died last night at home," one of them said.

"Alone in bed," added the other. "What is the state of his estate planning?"

"It was all settled, except for the stupid treasure hunt," Moira said. "We were still trying to agree to the terms of that with him. But that money needs to be recovered."

"Did he settle what we were entitled to?"

"Yes, as his heirs, you are left with one hundred thousand."

"Each?"

"To split," Moira said. "The rest is going to charities, foundations, et cetera."

"How much is the treasure hunt money? What happens if we can't find it?"

"Five million," Elliot chimed in. "If we can't recover the funds, then they're gone, I guess. We just have to hope no one else starts to look for the funds as well."

"None of it was a good idea. I advised him of this," Moira said.

"He didn't tell anyone where the money is located?" one of them asked.

Moira looked at Claudia.

"What did he say to you yesterday, Claudia?" Moira asked. "You were probably one of the last people to talk to him."

"He wouldn't want any of you to find his treasure." Claudia laughed. This was the moment she had been waiting for. Shoving this in Moira's face was wonderfully satisfying.

"Does she know?" one of the cousins asked. "Did he tell you?"

"I don't have to answer that, right?" Claudia said to Elliot.

"Technically not. But if he told you, and you could get this sorted out for us, Claudia, it would be a really big help."

"Well, that's not what Mr. Abberline would have wanted," Claudia said.

"Gentlemen, I think we should end this meeting now and schedule another one once Claudia is feeling more helpful," Moira said calmly.

The call ended. Moira pushed Elliot into the corner and whispered to him while Claudia's coworkers scurried out of the room as quickly as they could. Claudia slowly gathered her things and left the room,

while Moira and Elliot bickered quietly in the corner.

Claudia sauntered back to her desk. A small group
waited for her.

"If you know where the old guy hid all that money,
you should keep it to yourself for a while," Bailey
said. "If you tell Moira, she'll find it and then mis-
place it mysteriously."

"And he hated her," Chrissy said. "It would kill him
knowing she ruined his treasure hunt. You have a lot
more integrity than I thought, Claudia."

They finally respected her. And all it had taken was
outright defiance and insubordination.

The others scattered as Elliot approached.

"I've never seen anyone stand up to Moira like
that," Elliot said.

"Well, I don't have anything to lose anymore."

"Oh, really?" Elliot chuckled. "Do you have another
job lined up I should know about?"

"Oh no, nothing like that," Claudia said. "Things
just feel different this morning."

"I like that," Elliot said. "I feel like I haven't noticed
you before. And this morning, I'm having trouble fig-
uring out why that is."

Claudia smiled.

"How would you like to join me for dinner
tonight? I know a nice French place a few blocks
from the office. We could walk?"

"That would be nice," Claudia said.

Elliot smiled and went back to his office.

Claudia headed for the bathroom to look at herself in the mirror and confirm she still appeared normal and not like a ghost. But when she got to the bathroom, the door wasn't the right door. She stared at the swinging door, trying to comprehend how it had managed to get there. The dull white door featured a small circular window, like a kitchen door for a restaurant; it was industrial and worn. Something about it felt off, perhaps even asymmetrical.

As Claudia stared at it, it swung open, and her coworker Margaret exited and flashed her a brief smile before walking past. Claudia considered the strange door cautiously. As she stood before it, the swinging door revealed a kitchen on the other side.

As the door was suspended open, Claudia briefly saw a metal table, a cutting board, and some kind of meat in a pile. A hum droned inside. A metallic tang hung heavy in the air, like pennies, almost masking the sweetness of pumpkins, cinnamon, and vanilla. It put a sour taste in her mouth.

Swish.

A heavier wave of the smell, hot and steamy. A collection of eyeballs in a large glass mixing bowl. A human foot. The hum growing louder.

Swish.

An electric mixer. A pile of curly intestines. Blood splashing on tile. Hot pennies.

Swish.

Movement. A high-pitched mumbling. Someone reaching for the foot. A plume of pink flour mid-flight.

The door wobbled in its frame before halting at last.

Claudia wasn't going in there. She fled back to her desk.

*

The day Benny was kidnapped, he had been teasing her the whole bus ride home. He did that every day. He was mean to her at recess and lunch and whenever the teacher wasn't looking. Claudia hated Benny.

As they got off the bus, Benny yanked on Claudia's ponytail. After the bus pulled away, she picked up a large stick and threw it at him. It hit him in the back of the head, but not hard. It made him mad, though. Benny charged Claudia and knocked her down. He plopped on top of her, hitting her face. That was when the white car drove up and the kidnapper ripped Benny off her, covering his mouth and dragging him into the backseat of the car.

Claudia had a bloody nose. She went home and told her mother about Benny hitting her. She didn't tell her about what had happened to Benny.

TUESDAY EVENING

Claudia sat with Elliot in a beautiful dimly lit French restaurant that catered to business professionals in the financial district. Everyone around them looked like they were enjoying a late business dinner or a social outing direct from the office, dressed in high-end business attire. Claudia was glad she was wearing her favorite outfit. She assumed since she was dead, she would be able to wear the outfit for eternity.

Elliot told her about sailing his boat, his favorite pastime. He talked about the boat before ordering, and during appetizers. He never mentioned a girlfriend or a dog or any other hobbies or interests. It seemed as though when he was not at work, he was with his boat. Claudia couldn't tell if the boat was his passion, or if he was just trying to impress her.

Claudia would have liked to have a boat when she was a child. Her mother loved the ocean, and she would have enjoyed sailing. Claudia had grown up poor, but even though they relied on charity and food stamps, Claudia's mother had loved her and cared for her, and made sure she was never hungry. Her mother had worked two jobs and extra shifts to put money aside in a college fund for her. She had wanted Claudia to be a part of this world, to belong in a restaurant like this, and to never have to feel poor again. Growing up, that was what Claudia had wanted too—and to pay her mother back once she was older. It had always seemed so unfair that they were poor, like a wrong that needed to be righted. Claudia had been determined to fix it.

Claudia had gone to college and gotten a degree as her mother wanted. She had wanted to help her mother financially and make her proud. She'd also wanted to help people and make a mark on the world. But she'd wanted to be wealthy as well. Law had seemed like the field where she could accomplish all that at once. But as the years continued, and she spent more time with Moira at her firm, she had become unsure. And she hadn't looked into any grad schools.

Claudia hadn't told her mother about the financial hole she had dug for herself, about how high her rent was, about how many credit cards she had. She couldn't. Her mother would have been too disappointed in her. And Claudia was too ashamed to admit it to anyone. Her mother would find out soon, but she wouldn't be as disappointed. It wouldn't matter to her now since Claudia was dead.

Finally, after their entrees were set on the table, Elliot switched topics. Claudia was surprised she could eat and drink. She hadn't felt hunger or thirst since she died, and she would have assumed ghosts wouldn't be able to eat, and the food would fall right through her. But maybe she was allowed some kind of last meal. The food didn't taste as it would in life; it was like the flavors were muted. It was still good, but not as good. The wine was just okay as well. But after finishing two glasses during Elliot's monologue about his sailboat, Claudia realized the alcohol wasn't affecting her. So, she ordered more wine and drank it quickly, pleased that finally, she could drink as much as she wanted without making a fool of herself. *It must be my final reward.*

A champagne cork popped. A woman wearing sweatpants, with her hair in a messy bun, flashed through Claudia's mind. Blood stained her white t-shirt. She was trying to crawl away from something she was staring at behind Claudia, but she didn't make it far.

"So, I've been thinking of starting my own firm," Elliot said with a smirk.

"Really?"

"Do you like working for Moira?"

"Well . . ."

"You can be honest."

"Moira is the worst, and she hates me," Claudia said, finishing her fourth glass of wine. The waiter quickly replaced her empty glass with a full one. Elliot chuckled.

"She hates everyone," he said. "But she shouldn't hate you. You've been nothing but an asset to us."

"Really?"

"Definitely. And I'm sorry I haven't said anything before. If I had known you felt like that, I would have made sure you knew how much we value you."

"Well, thank you," Claudia said. "And I've been thinking of applying to law school myself."

"Oh, really? Well, if I start my own firm, I'll need good people I can trust to come with me. You can start with me as a paralegal until you finish school."

"Really?"

"It's hard to find people you can trust. And you've shown you can be trusted."

"Thank you."

"And if we find the treasure together, well, with that start-up money, we could do anything we wanted." Elliot smiled at her.

"That would be nice," Claudia said. It pleased her to play along with his little game. If she were still alive, she would be considering his offer.

"But Moira will be pissed at me and try to ruin

everything when she finds out, so it has to be a secret. So what do you say?"

"You're offering me a job?"

"And an adventure! Can I trust you?"

Claudia smiled at Elliot in the dim light. As she stared into Elliot's eyes, about to answer him that, of course, he could trust her, the lights dimmed even further. It was getting too dark. How was this happening? Were Claudia's eyes breaking down? As her body rotted, would her ghost start decaying as well? It was pitch-black now. But Claudia could hear Elliot talking and the waiters moving around as though nothing was out of the ordinary. Then a faint light shone in the darkness. She got up to go look at it.

"Where are you going?" Elliot asked.

"Be right back," she said, her arms out in front of her as she bumped into people and tables gently, apologizing profusely.

She followed the light, which was moving now. It seemed like she was in a tunnel. The light grew brighter; she'd almost made it.

Claudia turned a corner and entered a large dark room illuminated with hundreds of candles. Past the light of the candles, it was too black to see the shape or size of the room, like a deep cavern. She could hear the soft noise of candles popping and flickering as they burned. The small sounds echoed in the space.

Drip.

Drip.

Drip.

In the center of the room, illuminated by a circle of glowing candles, a tall naked figure stirred a metal spoon in a large cauldron. His flesh seemed loose, like it was hanging off his frame. Claudia realized it was sagging slowly, like he was melting from the heat of the cauldron. The drips echoing in the cavern were his liquified flesh splatting to the floor. There were gentle flames burning at the tips of his fingers, each one a tiny taper candle. The cauldron itself had a wide candle underneath it with many wicks all ablaze, warming it like a fire. Something hot and orange bubbled inside the iron vessel. Claudia didn't want to get any closer and see what horrors he stirred in his pot.

Drip.

Drip.

Drip.

He stirred with a gentle rhythm, and when he looked at Claudia, his face appeared like a mess of wax that had been smooshed together, barely leaving behind the features of a face. A soft yellow glow came from two holes where his eyes would have been. Melting flesh split in place of a mouth and the wax man spoke from the gash.

"I hope when you choose, you choose me," he said.

Then all the candles went out at once as the forceful gust of a foul-smelling wind roared through the cavern, plunging Claudia into total darkness. She yelped and turned to run somewhere, anywhere. She collided with two young women in a hallway of the restaurant.

"Sorry," Claudia said as the women sneered at her on their way into the restroom.

The light was back to full brightness. She made her way back to their table and found Elliot eating a steak. Elliot stared at her expectantly as she perched on the edge of her seat.

Something inside Claudia tugged at her, urging her back toward the strange room. Whatever these beings, these places were, they wanted her. They weren't going to stop. And Claudia worried that soon she would walk through a door she wouldn't be able to walk out of. If she stayed here, they would eventually come back. She needed to be somewhere safe. The doors were meant for her, but there had to be other options. She needed to get home. She needed to get out of here right now.

"Of course, you can trust me," Claudia managed to stammer while she stood up from the table abruptly. Her mouth tasted sour and sweet and tangy, as though she had sucked on a rusty nail. She raised her wineglass to her lips and poured down the rest of the wine, trying to get the taste out of her mouth. "But if you'll excuse me, I have to get home now."

"Why, was it something I said?"

"Oh no, you're lovely. Truly wonderful," Claudia said, already turning to leave. "But I can't be away from my body for this long."

Claudia ran for the door. Behind her, Elliot said "What?" and asked a passing waiter for the check.

Claudia hurried home. She needed to get to her body. She needed to check on it. She felt like a mother who had left her child home alone for the first time. Anything could have happened to her body. She had to make sure it was okay, even though that didn't make sense. Her body was dead. The worst had already happened.

Claudia felt silly for not telling Elliot she was dead. But pretending she was alive was fun, and she wasn't ready to stop just yet. She worried if she told anyone she was dead, then the dream would end and the nightmare would begin. Perhaps she'd already seen a glimpse of that behind the doors.

Claudia made it back to her apartment in record time. She opened the door and sighed with relief when she saw her body. It was right where she had left it, in the same place she had fallen and bled to death the night before. But as she looked at it more closely, a moan escaped her lips.

A fly buzzed and landed on top of her body's

splotchy gray skin. Her dead milky white eyes stared at nothing. Other fluids that hadn't been there last night stained the carpet. A new smell spoiled the air too. Being dead and seeing your body was one thing; witnessing your own decomposition was quite another.

Claudia took off her pink blazer and draped it over a chair. She found a raincoat in her closet and put that on over her cream dress. Claudia wasn't sure if she could stain her ghost outfit, but she didn't want to take the risk.

Claudia picked up her dead body. It was so much easier than it would have been for her in life. Did she have some kind of spirit strength? She carried her corpse to a closet. Her body had gone stiff, so Claudia had to lean her body upright in the closet, almost like one would stand up a broom. She closed the closet door. Her body would be safer in there, she told herself. And now she wouldn't have to watch herself rot.

Claudia took off the raincoat and put her blazer back on. She didn't have to eat or drink or sleep. So, she wouldn't. Claudia sat on her couch and gazed out the small window in her living room.

She let her mind wander until her thoughts almost ceased, staring out into the dark nothingness of the quiet night. She began to moan again, long pitiful gasps.

*

When eight-year-old Claudia was on the ground, with Benny beating her, she couldn't see the strange man until he pulled Benny off her. The man she recognized as her neighbor, Mr. Jacobson. He was an older father figure in the neighborhood, with two children off at college. Claudia hadn't known him well but had seen him around, including at the yearly summer block party. He seemed like a nice man before.

He pulled Benny off Claudia and told him to knock it off as he dragged him into the car. The white car sped off out of the neighborhood with Mr. Jacobson and Benny in the backseat, even though Mr. Jacobson lived only a few houses away from the bus stop.

After, Claudia would sometimes see Benny in the windows of Mr. Jacobson's house, staring down at her as she walked down the street. She wasn't sure if he was a prisoner or a ghost. After a while, Claudia believed Benny was a ghost and that Mr. Jacobson had killed him.

WEDNESDAY

Claudia watched the sunrise again. She had so rarely seen the sunrise in her life. Regret plucked at her; she hadn't seen as many sunrises as she could while she was alive. It was one of many regrets.

Claudia glided into her bedroom and looked in the mirror. She gasped. She still glowed, but with a stronger light than yesterday. But her neck was gone now, a see-through patch of space between her shoulders and her floating head. It was strange and startling, seeing part of herself had disappeared.

Today would be her last day at work. She could feel it. She tried to take off her blazer and found she couldn't. Her hands just slipped over it like it wasn't there, like it was a part of her now. Could she still put clothing on? She picked out a pink silk scarf from her closet and tied it around where her neck should have been. It mostly obscured the empty space. This was her ghost outfit for good, then. Claudia didn't mind. She wouldn't be able to pretend she was still alive for much longer, anyway.

People in the office noticed Claudia when she

came in this time. Chrissy looked her up and down and snickered.

"Late night with Elliot last night?" she whisper-hissed. "Nice scarf."

Claudia smiled. It didn't matter what any of them thought. Not anymore.

"What's in the bag?" someone else asked Claudia. She smirked and continued to her desk.

At her desk, Claudia opened one of the canvas tote bags she was carrying and removed a blender. She set it on her desk with a satisfying thud. Then she pulled out bottles of margarita mix, tequila, salt, and sugar. She grabbed the blender's cord and struggled to plug it into the outlet near her desk. She unplugged her desktop computer to make it fit. A small crowd had gathered around, watching her do this. Elliot walked past and did a double take. Moira stood in her office, peering through her window blinds. Elliot approached Claudia as she struggled to open one of the bottles of margarita mix.

"Here, let me help you with that," Elliot said, taking the bottle from her and giving it a firm twist.

"Thank you." Claudia smiled at him. He was very handsome. Would it be against the afterlife rules for a ghost to sleep with someone who was still alive? Maybe it would kill him.

"What's all this?" Elliot asked.

"I'm going to make margaritas for everyone in the

office!" Claudia looked around at her coworkers, who were still watching her and giving her odd smiles.

"At nine in the morning?" Elliot laughed.

"Better to start early," Claudia said. "It's something I've always wanted to do. I need to do it while I still have the chance."

"Oh, okay, sure." Elliot smiled. "Get ready for Margarita Wednesday, everyone," Elliot said to the crowd watching them. "Wait, Claudia, you don't have any ice here. Margaret, can you run out and get some bags of ice?" Elliot handed Margaret his company credit card. The rest of the group went back to their desks.

"So, what happened last night?" Elliot asked her in a hushed voice. "You took off all of a sudden. Was it the job offer or something else?"

Claudia fiddled with her scarf. Had he noticed, and was just being polite enough not to say anything about it?

"No, sorry. I . . . I had a lovely time with you. And I'm very interested in the job offer. I just wasn't feeling well, I guess."

"You did have a good amount of wine with dinner," Elliot said.

"And all this." Claudia gestured to the blender. "I guess I just feel like it's my turn to have a little fun now."

"Well, this will definitely piss Moira off," Elliot said. "So have your fun. It won't matter soon, okay?" Elliot gently took her hand in his and gave it a quick chaste kiss.

Claudia was surprised she could even feel his touch. Moira's blinds snapped back into place with a clatter. Elliot turned his head to look. He smiled at Claudia as he left her desk. He went into Moira's office, making a funny face at Claudia before he entered.

Claudia's coworkers returned with bags of ice. Once both the bosses were out of sight in their office, Claudia's coworkers got fully into her margarita plan. Claudia poured the mix into the blender. Then the tequila. The bottle glugged as she poured. Claudia remembered a young man on the ground in the frozen foods aisle the night she died. He'd been wearing a polo with some kind of company logo on the chest. He had been shot in the chest, making the logo unreadable. He'd sputtered and coughed and gurgled blood as he died, spitting little spatters and drops all over his face.

No one worked as they laughed and drank early-morning margaritas. Claudia smiled. Could it have always been like this? Claudia had three margaritas before 10:45. The rest of her coworkers were getting drunk, singing that Jimmy Buffet song, but the alcohol didn't affect Claudia. Moira peeked through her blinds at them, probably furious. But what could Moira do to her? Fire her, yell at her. Claudia was already dead. Moira couldn't hurt her anymore.

A few minutes before eleven, Moira exited her office with a newspaper.

"You all seem to be having a nice time." Moira attempted a smile, but it looked more like a wince.

"Would you like one?" Claudia asked. Moira glared at her before she remembered herself and the pained smile returned.

"No thank you," Moira said through gritted teeth. "But I did want to talk with you, Claudia, about this." Moira tossed a newspaper onto Claudia's desk.

Claudia picked it up and looked at the headline. "The Hunt is on for the treasure of Edward Abberline," she read aloud.

Her coworkers laughed, and a few high-fived. "Woohoo, Mr. Abberline!" "The old guy got what he wanted after all."

"The newspaper editor is an old friend of Mr. Abberline. Unbeknownst to any of us, he entrusted the friend with the clues to his treasure hunt and had the friend promise to publish that in the event of his death," Moira said, her eyes fixed on Claudia.

"Oh wow," Claudia said, spilling a little margarita on the newspaper as she looked over some of the clues.

"So now the clock is ticking, Claudia," Moira said,

her voice low and gravelly. "We have to find these assets before people get injured or injure others looking for this treasure. I'm not getting sued over some old man's weird pirate fantasy."

"You just want the money for *yourself*," Claudia said.

"Or maybe you want the money for yourself?" Moira said. "Come into my office and negotiate your terms. We can call it a finder's fee. I've had enough of this game."

Moira spun on her heel and flung open the door of her office. Claudia felt obliged to follow her. Inside, Elliot perched on the desk. Moira took her seat behind her desk, and Claudia sank into a chair, lounging almost gleefully. She had fantasized about telling Moira to go fuck herself for years. And now Claudia had something she desperately wanted. The tension in the office was exhilarating. Claudia had never had so much fun in her life.

Moira began lecturing her on legal obligations, her voice dry and cold.

In life, Claudia had craved money so badly. It had been all she could focus on. The life Elliot seemed to have—nice restaurants, fancy cars, a penthouse she had overheard some of her coworkers discussing—she had wanted for herself. And when she'd started to fail, when she hadn't gotten a good enough job, when she hadn't been sure about grad school, and she couldn't buy all the things she wanted unless she racked up a high bill on a credit card, it had just made her hunger for it more. That hunger gnawed at Claudia now, almost stronger than in life. She was a hungry ghost. Even though it no longer mattered, she wanted the money. She *needed* the money.

She would find it. It was hers.

Claudia blinked, the room becoming fuzzy and blurry. Claudia's head spun, light and floaty like she was about to faint. She couldn't see anything clearly, the office dissolving into streaks of colors and lights. But Moira still droned on about her obligations and this and that.

Suddenly, an open door stood beside Claudia; the refrigerator door from before. It was the only thing she could see clearly. Cold air flowed out of the doorway onto Claudia, filling the room with a chilly cloud. Claudia stood. She looked back and saw herself sitting in the chair. And she could still hear Moira talking as though she were still sitting there in the living world.

Claudia peeked into the refrigerated room. A woman stood in the corner with a panicked look on her face. She had on a white t-shirt and gray sweatpants, and her hair was in a messy bun.

"Help me," she said to Claudia.

As Claudia rushed toward her, the scarred man in the apron appeared, putting himself between Claudia and the woman in the sweatpants. He reached for the woman in the corner with his huge hand, pulling her out by her neck while she shrieked. She struggled and twisted her body to escape him, but his grip was too strong. With his other hand, he raised a heavy rubber mallet and slammed it directly onto the woman's head. Her eyes rolled up, the butcher let go, and she collapsed. Claudia covered her scream with her hands as the massive man picked up the woman and carried her to his table. Claudia spun to leave the room, but the door had disappeared. She was trapped.

He laid her out on the table delicately. He undressed her without ceremony, throwing her clothing over his shoulder and onto the floor. He retrieved his cleaver from where it hung on the wall. He began to chop the woman up methodically, unbothered by the blood that splashed on his body as he worked. There was a horrible rhythm to it that filled the cold room like a heartbeat. What had once been a woman, slowly turned into a pile of smaller, unrecognizable parts.

He flipped a switch and a meat grinding machine growled to life. He then fed the parts, piece by piece, into the rusty meat grinder. The machine ground her up in almost an instant. Then he separated the resulting meat into two piles. One pile he made into sausages, and the other he shaped into burger patties.

As he picked up the plates of patties and sausages, a door formed in front of him. He trudged through it and left the door open behind him. Claudia followed.

Everything was different on the other side of the door. The walls of the large room had been painted sky blue, and artificial green grass covered the ground. The plates of sausages and patties lay on a picnic table. Beings lurked in the room with Claudia. They were tall and gray, with no features, almost like they had been crudely shaped out of clay. There were larger ones and smaller ones, almost mimicking adults and children. They wore tattered, old-fashioned summer clothes. They didn't move but were frozen in various poses.

Sizzling broke the silence. A gray person manned an old charcoal grill with burgers and sausages cooking. As the meat cooked, a savory charred scent drifted through the room.

Something moved by the picnic table.

It was black, with a round white face, and a large unmoving grin with pointy black teeth. The being floated over the table and then in front of the gray people, who seemed not to notice it. Its long black arms and legs hung limply and looked like nothing more than empty fabric. The creature floated toward Claudia, its long arms and legs dragging on the ground.

"The end is coming," it whispered to Claudia, grinning. Its breath smelled sweet but rotten. Its round white face glowed ever so slightly.

"Follow your path with me," it said, the smile unwavering.

Claudia screamed and pushed its face away. It was hard and smooth, like plastic. The moment she did, she was back in her chair in Moira's office. Moira stopped talking and stared at her.

"Claudia—"

"I'm sorry, but I have to go!" Claudia shouted as she yanked open the office door. "The angel of death is after me! You wouldn't understand!"

As Claudia ran out of the office, Elliot muttered to Moira, "She's just drunk."

Claudia raced home and locked the doors and windows. She wasn't sure she could keep the angel of death or whatever that thing was out of her apartment, but she felt more secure here. It would return for her. And she had the feeling it wasn't planning on taking her somewhere nice. Otherwise, why would it be so scary? Claudia had grown okay with being dead, but she wasn't okay with going to hell.

*

Claudia never told anyone Benny had been kidnapped and murdered by her neighbor Mr. Jacobson. She was afraid if she told on him, he would kill her too. She had also hated Benny, and Mr. Jacobson had saved her from him. Maybe he had killed Benny to protect her, and the least she could do was keep it a secret.

Since Claudia never told, it was like it had never happened. It was like Benny had never existed. Claudia never acknowledged anything with Mr. Jacobson, no knowing glance or nod, no extra friendliness. It was like nothing had happened at all. No one talked about Benny or mentioned him ever again.

WEDNESDAY AFTERNOON

It was late in the afternoon when someone knocked on Claudia's apartment door. The thuds made her think of the cans falling from the grocery store display as someone crashed into them, attempting to escape the gunman. People tripped on the cans underfoot as they ran. The cans hadn't been the loudest noise. The gunshots and the screaming had been louder, but Claudia remembered the thunks of cans toppling so clearly.

She had been sitting on the couch, staring into nothing, since she got home from work. She had fled the office. The tips of her fingers on her left hand had disappeared now too. She could still pick things up, and feel with the now invisible fingertips, but it would be harder to conceal she was a ghost and was disappearing. She knew now she would never see her office building again. She couldn't go back. And that was okay. It felt strangely sad but good, like the last day of school. But Claudia had needed a moment to grieve. It was like she could almost put herself in hibernation when she wanted to. Then nothing else existed but the heavy emotions that engulfed her like she was underwater.

Claudia was surprised she didn't feel the need for constant entertainment or stimulation anymore. She liked the quiet now. The thought of turning on the TV or even listening to music was too much for her. Maybe that was what the promise of the afterlife was. An undisturbed time spent in a quiet room. She had just needed to let her spirit rest a bit before her journey. She should get ready to go, but she was tired. Not in the way she'd gotten tired in life. It was like her mind just needed to not be in use while her spirit worked some things out.

The knocking got loud enough to disturb her.

"Claudia!" Moira shouted. Then she murmured something, along with another voice. Claudia looked out the peephole. It was Moira and Elliot.

"Claudia!" Moira shouted again. "I know you're in there! I hope you've sobered up, because you need to tell me what you know. NOW!"

Then more murmuring.

"Hey, Claudia, this is Elliot. It seems like you might be going through something. Do you want to open the door so we can talk about it?"

"We can make a deal," Moira shouted. "What about that raise you were demanding?"

Was now the time to tell them she was dead? But she was worried about opening the door. She didn't want them to smell her dead body in the closet. She didn't want them to come in and see how she had been living. She didn't want them to barge in and mess everything up when it was almost going right.

Moira began to threaten to sue Claudia if she didn't tell her the location of the treasure. Her threats made Claudia laugh.

Claudia jolted as her apartment faded away. As it seemed like she was about to be in an empty white room, a kitchen gradually appeared around her, overlapping her living room. A young man with a polo shirt with a logo was sitting on the blue-and-white checkered linoleum floor of the kitchen, crying. He looked up at Claudia, reached out to her, and cried harder. His cries echoed in her mind. She had heard his whimpers before. Had he reached for her like this as well? Claudia stayed still, frozen in time and memories. She didn't take his hand; she didn't even reach out to him.

A small creature, only as high as Claudia's knee, wearing an oversized baker's hat, approached the crying man with a knife. The little baker was nude, with beady black eyes, pink skin, and a pinched face. He resembled a large hairless hamster. With his oversized blade, he cut off the man's hand easily, like he was cutting through a stick of butter. The man screamed and cried harder, holding onto his wrist. The little baker put the hand in a mixing bowl. The mixer sputtered to life, and in a second the hand was pulverized into a red powder that made a cloud in the air.

The baker continued cutting off parts of the man and making them into fine red flour, ignoring Claudia completely. Once the man had been all used up, and his screams silenced, the baker continued the mixing. He added cups of milk and sugar, tasting the batter periodically with tiny clawed fingers, until he had a nice pink batter. Then he poured the batter into a muffin tray and put the tray in a huge oven. The smell of baking filled the room: vanilla, sweet, earthy, and metallic.

"It only hurt for a little bit, he was mostly just sad," the baker said to Claudia over his shoulder in a high-pitched voice. "He's okay now. He'll even like it soon."

Claudia backed up and tripped over something behind her. As she fell, she found herself somewhere new.

It looked like a church basement. Everything was beige, and some crosses hung haphazardly on the walls. Cupcakes covered a buffet table to one side. The cupcakes were a pink cake with whipped white icing and a red drizzle. And each cupcake was garnished with a human eyeball placed in the center of the frosting.

Two tall nude figures who barely looked human-shaped stood near the table. One of the gray figures held a smaller gray figure like a baby. It wore a white lace gown and bonnet. The baby was the only one who moved. It held one of the cupcakes. The gray clay on its face split just a little to form a mouth, and it gnawed on the cupcake, covering itself in icing and scattering pink crumbs everywhere.

Fear pricked Claudia's spine like electricity. She had to get out of here.

"CLAUDIA!" Moira shouted.

The room around Claudia began to fade. She could see her apartment underneath the transparent scene with the cupcakes.

"Go away!" Claudia screamed.

"Tell us the location of the treasure!" Elliot shouted through the door.

"I can't tell you!" Claudia screamed. "I'm dead, and I can't tell you anything!"

"Claudia, we're going to go now, but we're calling the police," Moira said.

"For your own safety," Elliot added.

After they left, the church basement disappeared, and Claudia was back in her living room. Claudia couldn't stay here any longer. And she didn't have much time to get away. The smell of the bakery lingered in her apartment, sweet and rotten, savory and disgusting. It made her stomach growl. She wanted to be in the bakery. She wanted to eat, to consume whatever made that horrible, delicious smell. Claudia needed to feed the hunger in her ghost heart. She would have to give in eventually. But she had final business she must take care of before she could rest. The hunger was powerful, and she had to go now.

*

Years after the kidnapping, when Claudia was in high school, she was still racked with guilt and anxiety about what had happened. She asked her mother about Benny's disappearance.

"Mom, do you remember Benny Howard?"

"That boy who used to bully you? Of course I remember him."

"Did something happen to Benny?"

Her mother gave her a strange look.

"His family moved away. I remember the cupcakes we had in your class for him on his last day of school. I was room parent that day."

At her mother's words, it was as though Claudia could almost remember it. The memory was there, but it was blurry and far away. It created a strange dissonance in her mind. She was certain the last time she ever saw Benny, he was in the back of a white car. That memory was clearer, and it felt more real than the vague memory of cupcakes and being glad Benny would be gone soon.

Claudia's guilt didn't lift completely but was now mitigated by confusion and a sense of two opposing memories being true at once. Claudia accepted that it didn't make sense and was somehow true and not true at the same time. It was uncomfortable for her now, but not unbearable, like a pebble in her shoe. It only bothered her when she noticed it.

WEDNESDAY EVENING

Claudia went into the closet to get her body. At some point, her corpse had gone limp and had collapsed. The flesh of her body looked swollen and soft, a dark gray now. The smell was terrible. Claudia didn't want to touch the body anymore, but she had no choice. She scooped up her body and carried it down her apartment buildings stairs toward her parking spot on the street. She felt a tenderness toward her body, like it was a dead cat. It was important, but there wasn't much left she could do to signify its importance. It had been precious once, but not anymore.

Claudia carried her body to the car, setting it on the ground as she fumbled for her keys, trying to be as gentle as she could. As she got the car unlocked and the trunk open, she blinked down at her body's bare foot—she'd lost a shoe somewhere. She searched for the shoe, but froze. Moira and Elliot stood on the street, watching her.

"Are you going somewhere, Claudia?" Moira asked.

Claudia panicked and glanced down at her body on the ground at her feet. Moira smiled and took out her phone.

"She's calling the police, Claudia," Elliot said. "You should tell us what you know and where you're going."

Claudia stuffed her body in the trunk of her car as best she could. It was strange having to manipulate the corpse and fold the legs and arms so she could fit in the trunk. Claudia slammed the trunk and got into the car and sped away. She glanced in the rearview mirror. Moira yelled into her phone, with Elliot standing nearby. They didn't try to chase her. Claudia knew where she had to go.

*

Claudia arrived at a run-down lakeside motel in the early evening. It may have been a nice place to stay in the '70s or '80s but not anymore. The painted sign outside the motel was faded and hard to read, but it boasted lakeside views and family fun. The motel rooms all connected in a long strip. The exterior of the motel itself looked long overdue for a coat of paint, and moss grew in places on the roof. It didn't look warm or cozy or even insulated. Claudia frowned. Why were they open in the fall?

The sun was just starting to set as she checked in.

The motel office smelled damp and musty. Mounted fish decorated the walls. No one else seemed to be there but her and the slightly intoxicated man watching TV in the office, who barely looked at her when she checked in. Claudia kept her hand with the invisible fingers behind her back so the man wouldn't see.

The TV showed one of the victims of the grocery store shooting, a nice young woman in her midtwenties. Recently engaged. Beautiful, with long black hair. Her whole life had been ahead of her. Her fiancé cried for her on-screen. Claudia didn't want to look at her, but like the motel clerk, she couldn't look away from the screen. The tragedy of her short life was terrible and beautiful.

Claudia parked her car near her room and carried her body inside. She wasn't sure where to put it. She decided the bathroom would be the best place. When she tried to ease her body into the bathtub, she still managed to bang its head against the hard tub. The mouth hung open, and the lower eyelids seemed to sag. Claudia went to the bed and pulled off the sheet. She used it to cover her body.

It was getting dark now, and the sadness welled inside her. Maybe it was just a part of being a ghost. An unbearable sadness took control at night and made ghosts moan and howl. They were crying the only way they could.

Claudia was about to sit in an uncomfortable-looking wicker chair and start her ghostly moans when a tap on the wall started her. It was right above the bed, as though someone was sitting on the bed in the next room, tapping on the wall they shared.

Claudia mounted the bed and began to tap back. A knock answered her. She knocked back. Then it was silent.

Claudia left the room. She opened the neighboring motel room door and walked inside.

She stood in the dark cave with the candles. The melting man still stirred his pot.

"Would you bring that to me, my dear?"

Claudia looked around to see what he was talking about. A severed hand lay at her feet. The nails were manicured and painted pink. A diamond engagement ring glittered on the ring finger.

Claudia picked up the hand and brought it toward the melting man and his pot. It felt heavy and the skin was waxy.

"Toss it in here," he said.

She threw it into the pot and peered in. It looked like thick molten wax, a warm ivory color. The hand seemed to instantly melt inside.

"Thank you."

Claudia couldn't tell if he was smiling or not.

The candlelight flickered, and all of a sudden Claudia stood in a candle-lit restaurant. Dingy white tablecloths covered the tables, each with a long taper candle burning brightly at its center. Claudia stared at the candles. They weren't long, smooth candles like she would expect. These taper candles had skin-like creases and bony knuckles. And each impossibly long candle had a fingernail at its tip, burning with a small flame. Gray figures sat at the tables. In the center of the restaurant, a gray figure knelt on one knee, seemingly proposing to another gray figure. The one proposing held the engagement ring that had been on the hand in the melting pot.

The angel with the floating black body and the round white face drifted up from behind the couple, its unmoving grin fixed on Claudia.

"Hello, Claudia," the whispering voice of the angel of death said. "Your end is coming soon."

"Why are you chasing me?"

"Keep your voice down," he whispered. "We wouldn't want to disturb them." He looked around the room, but no one moved. "You're running out of time, Claudia."

"Well, I know that! Why are you trying to scare me?"

"You've been marked. I can see your path to death."

"Can't you just leave me alone?"

"You don't have much longer."

"Why not?"

"That terrible sadness you feel? I can make that sadness go away."

"What happens to me then?"

"You have choices to make first," the angel whispered. "You can float with me into nothingness, where your consciousness will cease to exist. Or you can choose the butcher, the baker, or the candlestick-maker."

"What? Why would anyone choose them?"

"Some souls are full of guilt, regret, and shame when they die. They want punishment. Or they want to continue to exist. Some people can't seem to let go."

"So, I can choose to be punished or I can choose to no longer exist?"

"Those are your options."

"Well, I don't like either of them."

"Why not?"

"I'm afraid to not exist. It's like I can't even understand the concept of it. How could I not exist anymore? How could I choose that for myself?"

"It will be peace, it will be quiet. It will be nothing. It's not that bad. You'll like it."

"How can I like it if I don't exist?"

"It's not that bad."

"And the others? The pain?"

"It's only bad for a little while. Then I've been told it's kind of nice in a funny way."

"I'm not ready to choose yet. I need to take care of my body."

"Of course," the angel chuckled. "You have a little time left. Tend to your unfinished business. Then I'll be back."

Claudia went back to her room. Tomorrow, she would bury her body. She would have a funeral and everything. And she knew exactly where her final resting place would be.

The treasure had always been for her. She couldn't use it now, but it would be hers. It would sate her horrible ghost hunger. It would make her feel better. It would make the ghosts' sadness go away. Then she would rest in peace. Then she could choose peace.

*

The events of the day Benny was abducted changed over the years as Claudia grew older. It was like she couldn't get the memories to fit together in a way that made sense. She still believed it had happened, or something like it had happened. Whatever exactly had happened, she believed Benny was dead.

Claudia wasn't sure why she had decided to look him up the week before she died, but she had. She had found Benny, alive and well on Facebook. And she was certain it was him. She recognized his parents in the family pictures he had posted. But even as she examined the pictures, proof of Benny living his life and growing older, she couldn't see anything but the ghost of him as a child. Benny would always be dead to her.

THURSDAY

The next day, Claudia drove to a hardware store and bought a shovel. She also stopped at a florist's shop and bought armfuls of flowers. She rented a boat from the motel manager—it would be nice to have one last day on a lake before the funeral.

In the motel room, Claudia laid out the sheet that had covered her body in the bathtub, and gently laid her corpse on top of it. She wrapped her body in the sheet.

Claudia dragged her body to the boat waiting in the water in broad daylight and lifted it inside. It was a crisp, slightly chilly day, but Claudia didn't feel the cold. The man in the office watched her through the window, but he didn't seem scared or concerned. She waited for him to pick up the phone and call the police, or come out and try to stop her, but eventually, he left the window.

The lake was large, with a cluster of small islands here and there. She wasn't ready to look for the island she needed to find yet; she just wanted to spend the daylight hours in the boat with her body.

Claudia let her mind go silent, and they sat there in the boat, gently bobbing for hours. She didn't want to think about what had happened at the grocery store, but it came in flashes. Screams, shouts, panic, and chaos. Claudia couldn't remember now what she had done in the moment. She couldn't remember how she had gotten out of the grocery store.

When the sun was beginning to set and the sadness encroached, Claudia rowed faster, searching for the island. Her fourth choice was correct. It was a small island, which she almost didn't see because it was obscured in a bend of the lake that made the whole area easy to miss. The island was overgrown with trees and brambles, and she couldn't see the run-down cottage she knew would be there.

They had gone over and over Mr. Abberline's assets at work. Out of curiosity, she had studied the maps of land and homes he owned. When he told her about the treasure on the lake, she'd known exactly what he meant.

As she rowed the boat closer to the island, she felt in her ghostly heart this was the right place. She landed the boat on the bank of the island and tied it to a tree. Then she picked up her body. Though she struggled to maneuver through the trees and the brush, she found the cottage easily in the center of the island.

The cottage was barely a house anymore. All that

remained was the wooden frame, a few portions of walls, and the stone fireplace and chimney. Claudia set her body in front of the house and trekked back to the boat to get the shovel and the flowers.

Claudia would bury her body on top of Mr. Abberline's treasure. Then it would be hers. It would be as though she had claimed it in death. Maybe she could even put a curse on anyone who took their treasure. Once it was hers, her terrible hunger would stop.

The safe was buried in front of the door of the house, and the passcode was Mr. Abberline's birthday. Claudia began to dig.

She found the safe as it was growing dark. It was huge, larger than she would have thought. But then Claudia hadn't realized how much space five million dollars would take up. She punched in the code. The door unlocked, and she opened it.

Then Claudia was somewhere else. She was sitting at a large dining room table. Gray figures sat all around the table with her. In the center of the table lay a large turkey. No, not a turkey—a human body that had been basted and roasted in the shape and position of a Thanksgiving turkey. A human head faced the opposite end of the table. It was Mr. Jacobson, her neighbor who she had believed killed Benny. He was the dead one now.

The gray figure at the head of the table began to move with slow, jerking motions like he was a puppet or an animatronic. And it looked like he was only miming the actions. Yet somehow, as he jerked the knife over the roasted body of Mr. Jacobson, slices of flesh appeared on plates all around her. Then the gray figures grew mouths, and they began to eat the meat.

"Are you hungry yet?" A voice from somewhere said. It sounded like it was coming from Mr. Jacobson's decapitated head. But the head didn't move or open its eyes. Claudia looked at the human turkey slice made from Mr. Jacobson that had been placed on the plate in front of her. She felt her stomach urge her to take a bite.

Claudia got up from the table. She was back on the island, sitting on the ground, a mound of dirt all around her. The door to the safe gaped open. She gasped. Cash filled the safe. It was here, the treasure. She smiled, overjoyed, but she was still so hungry.

She had just wanted to be comfortable, but it had grown into cravings of excess—her apartment, the mountains of clothes, all of it. She had been so close, almost there.

Much of her life had been spent worrying about money. About emptiness, about having nothing. Here it was, the answer to it all, laid out before her. And like Mr. Abberline had worried about, she was alone. Empty and alone and with no one coming to greet her. No way to keep the fortune. Her life had been a waste of wanting and consumption. She still felt hungry. Terribly hungry. The money didn't make her feel better. She still wanted, she still craved, and she didn't feel fulfilled or complete. She no longer had unfinished business, but she had nothing else either. There was no peace for her here. She moaned in a high-pitched wail that turned into a shriek that echoed across the lake.

She lowered her body into the grave, directly on top of the safe. She hoped Mr. Abberline wouldn't mind sharing his legacy with her. It was a small consolation. Being remembered did feel important.

Claudia scattered half of the flowers throughout the grave. She said aloud the words that came to her, hoping the eulogy she gave herself was good enough. She began to moan. It was hard to be dead, she understood that now.

She began to bury her body and the safe. When she was done, she laid more flowers over the fresh dirt.

*

Claudia would never figure out what had happened to Benny and why what she remembered wasn't what had happened. The mystery would never be solved, but it was over now. With her death, it didn't matter anymore.

THURSDAY EVENING

Claudia wanted one last sunrise. She left her grave and went back to the boat. She pushed off and rowed a little way away. Then she cleared her mind and waited. She would spend the night on the lake, waiting for the sun. Just one more time.

But fog rolled in. It had grown cold now, but Claudia didn't mind, unable to feel the chill. The fog surrounded the boat, obscuring the shore and the trees, the island where her body and treasure were buried. She reached into the fog, and her hand disappeared. She reminded herself this was coming. Soon she would disappear for real. The hunger inside her writhed and raged against the idea. It wasn't fair. She shouldn't have to disappear.

Tall, lanky, misshapen figures began to appear in the fog. It was like they somehow stood on the surface of the water. Claudia looked over the side of the boat. The grinning white face lurked just under the water's surface. The black fabric arms shot out of the water, grabbing her and pulling her over the side into the depths of the lake.

Claudia found herself at a birthday party. She was seated at a table with a dingy white tablecloth. Small teal plates lay in front of every chair, along with teal paper napkins. Around the table were small gray figures the size of children propped up in the chairs. They remained still. Taller gray figures stood against the wall behind the little ones. They all wore party hats. A TV on a stand in the corner of the room turned on, like the ones Claudia had known in school. The kitchen on the screen was blurry, the picture quality terrible. A VCR blinked on the stand under the TV.

The angel of death floated up from under the table.

"I wanted you to see a glimpse of what could be. Of what's to come."

A large older man hobbled onto the screen. He was naked. He looked familiar, but Claudia wasn't sure who it was until he spoke. It was Mr. Abberline.

"Who are you?" Mr. Abberline screamed at something off-screen. The little baker scurried across the screen and collided with Mr. Abberline. He swung something, and in one quick slash, Mr. Abberline's head was sliced off. It fell to the floor with a thunk, followed by the rest of his body.

The baker picked up the head and set it on a table. Claudia couldn't tell if the eyes were open or not, and she could only make out a pool of blood forming on the grainy black-and-white footage.

The baker lifted Mr. Abberline's decapitated body onto the table. First, the baker removed his arms from his shoulders. Then his legs. The baker cut the arms into small pieces, cutting through the bones as if they were nothing. The legs were next. The baker sliced the torso into cubes like it was as soft as a large piece of cheese. He tossed all the pieces of Mr. Abberline into an impossibly huge stand mixer that took up almost a quarter of the room, then emptied bags of sugar into the mixing bowl as well. A large sharp whisk began to mix the concoction.

The baker monitored the consistency of the batter in the bowl, adding more ingredients as needed. When he was satisfied, he ladled the mixture into round baking trays—Claudia counted six. He hoisted the trays into a huge oven. The sweet scent of hazelnut began to suffuse the room, and a warmth filled Claudia that she hadn't felt since she died. The oven dinged, and the baker arranged the six layers on top of each other, making a towering cake. The baker frosted each layer meticulously, piping *Happy Undead Birthday* over the large expanse of the cake.

The angel turned off the TV.

"It should be out any moment now. It should be to die for!"

A gray clay figure brought out the cake on an enormous teal platter. A second figure behind him brought out Mr. Abberline's severed head. They placed the cake and the head on the table. One of the gray figures put candles on the cake. An accordion rendition of the birthday song played on tinny-sounding speakers overhead. Something unseen blew the candles out. Then a gray figure began to slice the cake and place the pieces in front of the gray children.

Mr. Abberline's eyes were closed, but as the cake was cut, tears began to trail down his cheeks. They didn't stop. Claudia wasn't sure how she knew, but she was certain Mr. Abberline could feel what was happening to the cake and that it hurt him very much. He knew she was there too. And he knew what she knew, that his treasure hunt was already over.

Claudia looked at the slice of cake set in front of her. It was terrible and beautiful, and it repulsed her, but she couldn't help herself. She picked up a fork and took a bite. It was sweet and mealy, like cake and meatloaf together. She was so hungry. The taste just made her hunger worse. She wanted more.

Her stomach turned, and she stood up from the table. When she did, she was underwater. She swam to the surface and hauled herself back into the boat. She rowed back to the island. She wasn't sure why, but she went into the abandoned cottage and sat in front of the fireplace as though she was in her own home, escaping the cold outside. It felt like the right thing to do.

She let her mind go. The moans escaped her mouth. Maybe she could just haunt this island forever.

FRIDAY EVENING

Claudia lay on the floor of a living room with a dirty teal carpet. A cardboard fireplace and a fake Christmas tree decorated the room. The candle-maker took tiny bone-shaped candles out of his large cauldron and set them on the branches of the tree.

"It's not as bad as you think," he said to her. "I would never let your light dim. Never, I would."

The candlemaker reached into the cauldron with both waxy hands and pulled out a head with a large wick coming out of the top of the skull. Claudia couldn't be sure, but the head looked like her father. The candlemaker lit the wick and placed the head on the top of the Christmas tree. Claudia's father's head began to melt with a lovely golden light.

"Don't you want to glow?"

Claudia tried to sit up, but she couldn't. She was back in the cabin, lying on the floor. Her muscles trembled as she struggled to move her body. How long had she been here? What was happening to her?

She hadn't been asleep, but she couldn't remember what had happened. It was like she had ceased to exist. She raised an arm. Her hand was see-through. She was beginning to completely disappear. She couldn't stay in the world much longer. She had given herself a funeral and buried her body, and now her time on earth was coming to an end.

And then her life began to flash in front of her eyes and she remembered. Everything.

*

Benny had made fun of her on the bus. He had yanked her hair, and she had thrown a stick at him. He had pushed her down and punched her. Their neighbor Mr. Jacobson had pried Benny off her and told him to stop. Then Benny had gone home, and Claudia had gone home and told her mom.

The next day, Claudia had gotten off the bus. A white car had driven up with the radio blaring. Her father had gotten out of the car. He'd told her Claudia's mother was mad at him, and he was going to stay somewhere else for a little while. He'd said he would call her. He had given her a quick hug and gotten back into the loud white car. A woman had been driving it. The car had sped out of the neighborhood. That was the last time Claudia had seen or heard from her father. A little while later, Benny's family had moved away.

The memories had gotten all tangled and confused

in her mind, and untrue elements had been added instead. Claudia didn't know why, but it was like as she was about to leave the world, everything was untangling in front of her. Things were being set right.

And then her memories advanced to the grocery store. The shooting. The woman in the sweatpants trying to crawl away, the man with the logo polo who spit blood and reached out to her. She had ignored them as she fled, hiding herself behind a display until the gunfire ceased. She watched it all again. But this time, it didn't seem as horrible. It couldn't hurt her anymore. It was almost like it wasn't real. She wasn't reliving it, just watching it, and taking in the information. She had heard the gunshots. She had hidden until the police came. She had evacuated the store. But she hadn't been shot. When had she been shot?

Claudia never had been shot. She had driven home, and upon entering her apartment, her mind had fractured. She'd had a panic attack and passed out on her floor. She had woken up to a delusion that protected her from the truth. She could see it all now. This money could have been hers. She could have changed her whole life.

With the darkness all around her, she finally felt the numbing cold, the hollow cavern in her stomach, her sandpaper tongue and throat. Claudia struggled to turn her head toward the fireplace. Maybe if she could make a fire and warm herself? Maybe she could drink some lake water? No—it was too late now. Now, she was really dying.

Her vision ended. The angel hovered close to her face.

"You have to make a choice," he said. "You're out of time. You are going to die now."

The angel hadn't been trying to bring her to the afterlife, he had been showing her what death was like, what awaited her there. Once she thought she was dead, it was as though she'd marked herself for death. She was never going to escape this.

Claudia couldn't move. She tried to look at her hand again, but she couldn't lift her arm. The thought of being gone for good was terrifying. Fear shook her to her core. She was too full of sorrow and grief and hunger and fear. She didn't want to die again. She couldn't let go. She couldn't release herself of any of it. She didn't want to be gone. She didn't want to disappear. It wasn't fair; this life was hers. Claudia struggled to speak.

"The baker," she whispered.

Then she died. She closed her eyes, and everything disappeared. She floated alone in darkness like water, her consciousness free, detached from any physical form. Her emotions lessened. They were still there, but softer now, muted. Peace infused her. Finally.

*

Then she was back in her body, but also not in her body at the same time. She could see with her own eyes, but she could also view the whole room as though she was floating overhead. Claudia met the baker in the kitchen. She closed her eyes so she wouldn't have to look at him, but she still observed everything from above. Pain lanced into the top of her head, and she collapsed to the ground. The baker decapitated her, which was a quick, sharp sting, and then the pins and needles of numbness.

After she was decapitated, she continued to exist in her body. It was dark and she couldn't see, but she retained all her sense of touch—pain and pleasure. She could still feel everything. Claudia could watch the baker process her corpse, and she could feel all the pain as he sliced, ground, and mixed her body parts into a batter.

It took much longer than it had for Mr. Abberline. The baker was making Claudia into something big, something special.

Claudia found herself in a small ballroom. Everything was dingy white. A tarnished chandelier hung overhead. Gray figures filled the ballroom, some sitting at tables. Two stood near Claudia's table. One wore a stained white wedding dress, and the other a torn black suit. Claudia was a large multitiered white wedding cake with delicate red flowers adorning the sides. Her severed head served as the cake topper. Whipped cream covered her eyes, each topped with a cherry.

The newlywed couple cut the cake. Claudia was more than just the cake, she was everything. She was the ballroom: she could feel the chairs moving, the steps of the gray creatures trying to dance to accordion music. She inhabited the beings getting married and eating the cake. She was the guests. And she was the cake as well. She was all of it, and it hurt, being cut open and consumed, but it was also the funny feeling of being alive. Happy, nervous and loved. This wedding was for eternity now. It tingled and burned and was everything she could have wanted. And she was no longer hungry.

Famous Treasure Hunt Reveals Greater Mystery, article in the *Lakeview Herald*

One year after the death of Edward Abberline and the start of a notorious treasure hunt for his fortune that would leave three dead, the treasure has been found, but a greater mystery has been discovered.

A husband and wife team had researched the clues from the original newspaper release for months before they embarked on the treasure hunt. As professional treasure hunters, they said the clues and the mechanics of the hunt itself were poorly thought out. They believe Mr. Abberline picked the locations the clues led to, which led to more clues, because of their difficulty. The deaths from the hunt were of people lost in inaccessible locations not being found in time. The Baryards theorized that Mr. Abberline wanted people to get lost and perish, and said they had never been on a hunt that seemed to have so little regard for human life.

When the Baryards finally arrived at the small lake island, which was by far the safest, and least harrowing location, they discovered the abandoned cottage once owned by Edward Abberline. There they easily unearthed the safe that contained the fortune. They also stumbled upon a body in the cottage.

The body was eventually identified as Claudia Everly. She was an employee of the law firm Mr. Abberline had used to plan his estate. She had disappeared shortly after Mr. Abberline's death, and it was believed she had been aware of his treasure's location. So why was her body found in the cottage? Why hadn't she taken the treasure?

An autopsy on Ms. Everly's body determined she died from a combination of dehydration and exposure shortly after her disappearance. There was no evidence of injury or physical trauma. Her body appeared untouched. It was as though she had lain down and died. A boat was found that was identified as one rented from a motel where Claudia had stayed when she was last seen. Belongings were found in the boat that identified her as well. There was no evidence anyone was in the boat with Claudia, that she was murdered, or that she'd died by suicide. So why was Claudia dead after finding the treasure?

The mystery remains unsolved, and the Baryards felt the need to honor Claudia—the first to complete the treasure hunt— by giving Claudia's mother half of the five-million-dollar treasure.

"She won the treasure hunt. We can't know what happened after that, but she did get there first."

The theory that currently has taken hold of the treasure-hunting community is that Claudia's death was an accident. Perhaps she thought she could gather the treasure quickly and leave. Perhaps she spent the night attempting to think of what to do next. There were no traces that anyone had attempted to make a fire in the fireplace, even though during the evening theorized as the time of Claudia's death, the temperatures dipped below freezing. Perhaps Claudia hadn't meant to die; maybe she just hadn't been prepared to take care of herself in the cold, decaying cottage overnight.

However, the true-crime podcast, *What We Didn't Know Then*, has speculated Claudia was murdered. The general public has latched onto this theory, and are demanding a further investigation.

"Someone knows what happened to Claudia," Raleigh Greene, cohost of the podcast, commented online Sunday. "And that person is the reason she's dead."

Mr. Abberline's estate has denied any knowledge of the location of the fortune, as has his former attorney, Moira Caven. But many believe there must have been foul play involved. None of those people could be reached for comment before the publication of this article.

What has confused the mystery even more is a note written in Claudia's handwriting found in her purse. The list contains items found on the island with her.

"Shovel, flowers, wine, rope."

Why would she bring those things to the island to find a treasure?

Claudia's motivations are the biggest mystery here, and now that the Abberline treasure has been found, many are trying to solve the mystery of what happened to Claudia.

ACKNOWLEDGEMENTS

I'd like to thank my wonderful husband and my most amazing child for being loving and supportive. You are more than I could have ever hoped for. And I must thank all the scary people I've met on the internet for their continued support.

ABOUT THE AUTHOR

Mae MacCallum lives in a rural part of New England with her family. Mae is terrified of invasive technology and people on the internet. When not writing about the things that scare her, you can find her in her house looking out the windows at the trees and glaring at any neighbors that happen to walk by.

Thank you for reading Undead.

If you enjoyed this novella, please leave a review.

Follow Mae at https://maemaccallum.com

Follow Rotten Pumpkin Press at https://rottenpumpkinpress.com

&

https://www.instagram.com/maemaccallum

www.ingramcontent.com/pod-product-compliance
Lightning Source LLC
Chambersburg PA
CBHW031415310726
48971CB00003B/873